Probiotic

Psychotic

PUBLISHED IN CANADA BY MATT PAYNE
COVER AND INTERIOR DESIGNED BY MATT PAYNE

ISBN: 978-1-0697563-1-2

PATTMAYNE.COM

Probiotic

Psychotic

Contents

Larry Grank Saves the Kilogram....... 1

Bikesport..... 15

Werner Herzog in Space..... 47

Larry Grank and the Flat Earth..... 65

Haunted Chocolate..... 85

LARRY GRANK SAVES THE KILOGRAM

This story was published by Terror House Magazine in 2020, and again by Futurist Letters in 2025.

I received a letter in the mail, which was strange because nobody knows my address. I took the envelope inside, protected my body by donning a gas mask and gloves, and sliced the fucker open.

It was a ransom note, neatly typed on high-quality acid-free paper. The texture was so rich I was tempted to remove my gloves and caress it with my bare skin, but immediately recognizing the trap, I resisted the dangerous urge.

I read the message aloud and my voice was muffled by the gas mask. "Dear Larry. Deliver the Hammer of Vuvun or I'll steal the kilogram, sending your precious metric system into chaos."

I didn't have any Hammer of Vuvun, so this letter was barking up the wrong tree. But I buy my supplements and laboratory chemicals by the kilogram, plus all my analog scales and measuring equipment deal in metric, so I couldn't have this lunatic throwing that system into disarray (I always use analog because it's harder to hack).

I checked my trusty 1987 encyclopedia to confirm that the precise weight measurement of a kilogram is defined by a physical object, the International Prototype Kilogram, which (according to the encyclopedia) is a little metal weight stored at the International Bureau of Weights and Measurements in France. I immediately called their director.

"Somebody's planning to steal the kilogram unless I deliver the Hammer of Vuvun."

"I'm sorry, who is this?" the director asked.

"There's no time for that," I explained. "You have to step up your security pronto or we won't know what anything weighs anymore."

"Sir, the kilogram was officially defined mathematically in reference to the Planck constant in 2018. So it's a concept now."

"Measuring weight with a concept?" I repeated incredulously. "How much does a concept weigh?"

"In this case, a kilogram. The point is that nobody can steal a concept."

"But what if they could?" I asked.

"Well that would be...very bad," the director admitted.

"Maybe we should change it back to the physical standard, to protect the Planck constant. We can physically guard a physical object, but ideas are under constant threat of sophistry, bias, hallucinations, and fallacious reasoning."

The director scoffed. "I've been trying to get them to revert to the tangible Kilogram for years! They won't listen. They've got their heads in the clouds, obsessed with pure rationality and abstract forms, while the little guy, you and me, we toil away here in the physical realm. You and me, we know what's up, but the ivory-tower acolytes don't trust the unwashed masses with tangible measurement standards."

"Don't be so defeatist," I scolded him. "If we explain how vulnerable their ideas are in the post-truth era, they're sure to see their error. We could convene an Assembly of Measurements and pitch our case there."

"Nothing would make me happier," the director said. "The Bureau's shares plummeted when they switched the kilogram to a concept. But I've tried everything!

Blackmail, seduction, reasoned arguments, murder, begging, but nothing works!"

"Just bring them this new information, and in the meantime, I'll see if I can track down this Hammer of Vuvun. We'll reconnect tomorrow and share our progress."

"You got it. Talk to you tomorrow, Larry."

I hung up the phone and grabbed a different volume of my trusty encyclopedia. I searched high and low but found no reference to any Hammer of Vuvun. Naturally I don't have the Internet, because it can be hacked and somebody could trace me. So I added a green baseball hat and grey hooded sweater to my gas-mask-and-gloves and, replete in my disguise, I headed to a local Internet cafe. The Singaporean shopkeeper accepted my cash and I logged in anonymously. Then I searched for "Hammer of Vuvun" in my favorite search engine.

Various articles informed me that the Hammer of Vuvun was a rare piece of loot in a popular online video game where everybody is an adventurer and nobody is a peasant. It sounded suspicious to me, sounded like a scam, but I needed to get my hands on that hammer. The Singaporean shopkeeper accepted more of my money and I started playing the game, which was called *Realm of Adventurers.*

I've often speculated that real-life is itself a video game, or hologram, or simulation, so it felt very weird indeed to descend into this lower-level virtual world, like a virtual world within a virtual world. I only hoped that I would still be able to tell the difference when I emerged.

My first few hours in *Realm of Adventurers* were a gruelling spectacle of humiliation. The game's tagline turned out to be untrue, as I was clearly a peasant among warriors. My strength and stamina were nil, I was frequently bested by seasoned virtual veterans, referred to as a noob (and worse), and sent on endless banal errands which often resulted in my demise. I asked everybody about the Hammer of Vuvun, but received only scorn. I also made a list of the people who mocked me.

I played all through the night. By sunrise, I'd

accumulated lots of loot and experience points (not to mention enemies), but still not a single clue about the Hammer of Vuvun. In my exhaustion, I was almost ready to accept the imperial system. But then, I chanced upon a wise old witch sharpening her broomstick near the outskirts of a village, and I asked her about the hammer.

The witch looked up and down the path. There was nobody else in sight. "Ask the shopkeeper," she said through a little textbox.

"But we're not in a shop," I responded. We were out in the open virtual air, beside a creek which ran under a bridge.

"No, but you are," she said. Then she cast a spell and disappeared.

How could she have known that I was in a shop? I looked around at the other gamers, peering at their screens, but nobody else was playing *Realm of Adventurers*. After removing my headset, I approached the Singaporean shopkeeper. He was reading a weathered hardcover tome and vaping. He smelled like cinnamon. I leaned over his desk and whispered, "I need the Hammer of Vuvun!" The gas mask added gravelly gravity to my voice.

He must have been expecting me, because he pulled a card from within the pages of his book and handed it to me. On the card, pre-written in pencil, were the words, "You kill rats in basement. I give you hammer!"

Another menial task! In *Realm of Adventurers*, I had finally evolved into a real adventurer, killing orcs in haunted castles and defeating whole teams of bandits. But back here in the so-called real world, I was demoted to slaying rodents in the cellars of shopkeepers. What's worse, I had no real-life weapons except my wits.

"I have no weapon," I told him.

The shopkeeper reached beneath the desk and pulled out a rusty, battered sword. Alongside the sword was another card, which said, "You use bastard sword!"

The sword was extremely heavy and dull. I hefted it over my shoulder and went into the dank basement. Rats were everywhere, scurrying around on the cement. I had no personal qualms with these rodents, but I needed that hammer. So, instead of killing them, I found a cardboard box and used my bastard sword to try herding them inside. But it was worse than herding cats. They shredded the cardboard with their filthy claws and teeth, then arranged the pieces into words on the floor which spelled, "The Metric System is Rubbish."

Well, that was it. I smashed the little pests with my weapon, and I was glad the blade was dull. The metric system is the only thing that makes sense in this inexplicable world. The blade crushed their spines and skulls, splattered their brains and guts. They twitched in the dirt. Some fought back, trying to bite my legs, shredding my corduroy pants, but my antimicrobial Kevlar long johns protected me. Finally, they were all slain and I went upstairs to claim my prize.

The shopkeeper handed me a USB drive and a card that said, "Thank you."

I decided to test my bartering skills. "Is this it?"

The shopkeeper then handed me another card which said, "Well, I suppose you've earned a bigger reward." Then he handed me two gold coins. I added them to my inventory and exited the Internet cafe.

Back home, I checked out the contents of the USB drive. I found a single file containing a 3D model of a beautiful blue warhammer. It had a ribbed grip on a short handle and a heavy head inscribed with writing in an alien character set. In my 3D rendering program, I scrutinized the prize from every angle. Zooming in, I found even more detail, more inexplicable writing. I zoomed in even closer and found the whole hammer was perforated with tunnels, and those tunnels were lined with houses, trees, and little people reading books or tilling their gardens. The Hammer of Vuvun was a world unto itself. The writing inscribed on its surface was too small for me to see from a distance, but too large for these tiny people to see from their minuscule vantage point. No wonder the letter wanted this hammer so badly.

Still wearing my protective gas mask and gloves, I retrieved yesterday's threatening letter and showed it the hammer on the screen. "I got you the hammer," I told the letter. "Now what?"

But the letter didn't respond, and I didn't know who had sent it.

I decided to call the director to see how his progress had gone. But when I dialed his number, his secretary answered and informed me that she hadn't seen him since yesterday. "To be honest, we're pretty worried," she said. "His wife hasn't heard from him either. Should we call the police?"

"The police might be in their pocket," I muttered. My mind was searching for answers.

"Whose pocket?" the secretary inquired. "Is the director in trouble?"

I ignored her questions. "Do me a quick favour. Measure out a litre of water and tell me how much it weighs."

She quickly complied. "One kilogram," was her answer.

"Then we still have time. Has the director received any mail since he went missing?"

"Why, yes. There's a single unmarked envelope in his inbox."

"Put on a gas mask and gloves," I told her, "and rip that fucker open!"

Moments later, the secretary was breathing noisily through her own gas mask. Her muffled voice read the letter that she discovered within the envelope. "Dear Larry. I have your precious director. Meet me under the bridge in one hour, and bring the hammer!"

"Which bridge?" I asked.

"The letter doesn't say," the secretary answered.

I hung up the phone and put on some shoes. I was about to head out the door with the USB drive in my pocket, when I experienced an idea. "Maybe I should make a copy of the hammer," I mused. So I plugged the drive back into my computer and started printing the hammer with my 3D printer. It took 55 minutes to print, but finally, the Hammer of Vuvun was physically manifested. I left it on my kitchen table, pocketed the USB drive, and ran out to the nearest bridge.

It was a walking bridge running over a shallow creek. I had to crouch to fit underneath. My rat-shredded corduroy pants got wet up to my knees. A gang of children wearing lab coats and gas masks awaited me there wielding microscopes and digital scales. The director was there, looking exactly as I had imagined him: kneeling down, blindfolded.

"I brought the hammer!" I told the kids, holding the USB drive aloft.

One of the kids operated a remote control cargo boat, which drove over the water. The boat carried another envelope, and I ripped the fucker open. A letter inside said, "Put the hammer in the boat."

I wondered how much weight that little boat could carry. If the Hammer of Vuvun contained whole worlds within its perforated body, then it might be too heavy for the little boat. But that wasn't my problem.

"Release the director!" I yelled at them. "And I'll give you the hammer!"

One kid shoved the director. He stood up and bumped his head on the roof of the bridge, then bent over and started shuffling forward. I put the USB drive on the boat, and the remote-control operator made the vessel turn around and head back to the gang. But the boat was displacing more water now. Little waves sloshed over the little rails; the little motor struggled.

The boat sank just as the director stumbled into my arms. I tore off his blindfold. The kids were frantically typing a letter, but they had no way to deliver it to me.

"Let's get out of here!" I told the director.

"But the hammer sank," he protested. "They'll still try to steal the kilogram."

"Let them try," I said, pulling him out from beneath the bridge, ushering him up the shallow bank. "We can't live in constant fear of these terrorists. And after all, our scientific standards mean nothing if we don't protect our relationships. We still displace water. We still weigh *something*, no matter what! If we have to fight to protect our ideas and standards, then we'll fight! We won't let them hold our directors hostage anymore!"

We reached the path and sunlight shone on the director's face. "Maybe the kilogram lives inside all of us. Maybe we all are the kilogram."

Then we went to the Internet cafe and played *Realm of Adventurers*.

Bikesport

When Futurist Letters put out a call for fiction in a journalistic style, I sent them this story. They were nice enough to publish it. It's a series of fictional articles by fictional journalists documenting the fortunes of a dirt-bike team in Newfoundland.

Declaration of Tournament

by Alton Abernathy

After weeks of hiding in the thicket of these northernmost Appalachians I began to doubt the veracity of the tip that had sent me here. Maybe I was too excited, even gullible, when a toothless elder told me a tale about the strange men who host strange sporting events, attracting strange competitors. How they came from the darkest woods.

But then they appeared. From the flowing green depths of the muted nubs comprising the Long Range Mountains emerged three men in blue suits like fleas from a shag rug, and they entered into the town of Bikeminster. They found a telephone pole and upon that pole they posted a poster, and the poster read, "Bike Stunt Trick Tournament: winner gets free medical experiments: inquire within." Thereupon they constructed a geodesic dome, and entered into it, and waited for applicants.

Most of the locals were tight-lipped about who might compete. I needed to get to know the athletes, like I needed to document the crooked spirit of their culture. Ostensible Christians marinating for centuries in these undeniably pagan environs. But I found a few who told me the names of the Home Team, where they might be found, how they would surely travel. I found an elevation where a satellite signal made itself inter-mittently available, and I handed the information off to my colleagues.

Mister Mattias

by Vera Nottingham

At first I was skeptical about this assignment. The only thing worse than sports writing is travelogues. Especially travel in such a backwater province of this backwater nation. But beggars and journalists can't be choosy, and I'm nothing if not a team player, so I got my gear and hit the road.

My mood changed when I met the charismatic Mister Mattias, and the effect was only enhanced as we drove down the highway on his dirtbike. The bike growled and purred like a horny tiger and his mohawk was stiff and tugging at his scalp in the wind. Our leather jackets kept us warm on the cloudy day. The evergreens were fragrant and tangled. I spied jealous Paparazzi hidden in the thicket with their leering eyes snapping photos. This landscape grew on me. It seeped into my soul.

A siren turned the world psychedelic evil and Mattias deferred, pulled over onto the gravel which crunched in grumbling solidarity. A police officer motorcycle approached and its headlight eyes glared at us. The officer dismounted, and when he pulled off his helmet his eyes were pure static. He said, "Yiss b'y tell us how much of a bike belongs on a highway if it's dirt-style."

"Tis so," said Mattias. "I'm headin' out to meet me crew of five for a dirtbike championship in Bikeminster and I can't very well arrive if it ain't through the highway now is it?"

"I don't doubt it," the officer agreed sombrely. But then he tilted his head and the clouds parted slightly. He said, "Ain't you Mister Mattias, the gay dirtbike champion o' the world?"

Mattias coughed mightily, and confirmed that he was indeed.

"Well Mister Mattias I am certainly red in the face to hold up yer progress towards yet another conquest. But I am an officer o' the law, a mere mortal in service o' something I cannot comprehend. And this here dirtbike ain't highway material. I'm obliged to offer you a ticket, loathe as I am to do so. Tell me, does your beautiful bike got a name?"

Mattias answered, "I named him Horse."

The officer shook his head and scribbled a ticket. "Now listen. I'm gonna let you two off the hook for ridin' that dirtbike on the highway, call it a warning. But we all know this bike ain't no horse. It's a donkey. And from this day forth you will call him Donkey. And I'm writin' you a ticket for such a nomenclature infracture. And you must immediately remove Donkey from the highway and either walk him along the side o' the road or else ride him thru the impenetrable jungle of evergreen thistle and leering Paparazzi. I hope you don't get lost or swallowed, but she's outta me hands."

The officer winked at me without good cheer.

Into the gnarls and the thorns we rode upon Donkey the mighty dirtbike who took the indignation with dignity and fortitude. But it weren't the scratches what slowed us down, no sir, it was the blinding flashing bulbs of the Paparazzi creatures always in the shadows hiding behind the scratches, making molds of Mattias' face, mimicking his utterances like evil prayers. It stayed our progress, lo, unto less than a crawl, a halflife of movement ever diminishing yet never quite reaching zero, merely generating a uselessly decreasing infinity betwixt ourself and the ETA.

I suggested we make a deal with the Paparazzi. Mattias nodded and called out, "One interview I bequeath unto thee, thou heathen hordes."

A pretty girl appeared in a sudden clearing, and I was

jealous of sharing my scoop. She, starry eyed and stern of lip, spake, "Mister Mattias, why are you competing in the Bikeminster Bike Stunt Trick Tournament?"

Mattias answered, "Me mudder is badly in need o' medical experiments."

She wrote something down in her fuckin' little notebook. Then she said, "When did you first realize you were a gay dirtbike champion?"

"I suppose when I won me first dirtbike championship."

"So you already knew you were a homosexual?"

"On the day I was born I swore never to return to the womb."

She thanked him and the forest parted, offering us a path. Mister Mattias hawked up a wretched glob of blood-riddled phlem, and he coughed and coughed and spat it out. Then he revved his engine and we rode Donkey the dirtbike through the arboreal jungle, toward a rendezvous with his five-person crew.

Gloria McStepanovich
by Michael Tuck

Gloria McStepanovich allowed me to tag along on her journey. She arrived at the truck stop sporting a multi-colored explosion of twisted bantu knots. Her leather jacket was pink with black trim. I climbed on the back of her dirtbike which proceeded to gurgle down the highway at a meandering pace.

I asked why she was driving so slow. She said, "I'm looking for a particular bug. I can't win the Bike Stunt Trick Tournament unless I find this bug."

She told me the story of the bug:

Many years ago she had stood in the doorway of a darkened room, with the light behind her, casting her shadow on the wall inside the room. She knew the shadow was more than her doppelgänger. She approached it, wondering what the shadow had to say, maybe something to ask of her, maybe something to offer. When she was close, Gloria saw that there was a bug on the wall, on the shadow's heart, or maybe its brain, she couldn't remember which. But she knew that she had to eat the bug.

She knew that she must eat that bug.

But she did not eat the bug. Because eating bugs is gross. Possibly unsanitary. And maybe even cruel. One shouldn't assume that another would prefer to be devoured.

The bug remained on the wall for three days. On the fourth day it was gone, and she despaired that she would ever become her ultimate self.

Now her crew of five dirtbike stunt trick athletes was gathering for the Bike Stunt Trick Tournament, and she had to find that bug before she arrived. Find it and eat it. Maybe it was too late. She watched the roadside gravel for any little crawling thing, and studied the branches of the trees. She saw many bugs, but they were the wrong bugs.

Suddenly she screeched to a halt, her tires leaving a pink streak across the pavement. She pointed at a crack in the pavement and said, "It's bad luck to cross a crack in the road."

I suggested we pass around the crack, on the roadside gravel. But she answered, "What is gravel but one extremely crack-riddled rock?"

She knelt to pray. It was a long prayer but she recited it by heart, pleading for mercy in a world full of cracks, down to its molten core.

Then I saw it too. Just how many cracks there were, everywhere. The road was all cracked up for about twelve meters, resulting in many little islands, like tiles on a game board. Serenaded by her prayers, I saw so much that had been hidden to me before. These islands between the cracks, they could be represented as a collection of tiles, each tile with a numerical index. And Gloria's prayer promised to use only prime numbers. But if we stepped on a five, and then a seven, these two numbers added up to twelve, which was not a prime number (though twelve is represented with a one and a two, which add up to three, which is a prime number, so that's a mitigating factor). We would have to take many steps to reach the other side, and we needed to be sure that however we added the indices of our chosen tiles it would always add up to prime numbers whose digits also added up to prime numbers (it was okay for a prime number's digits to add up to a non-prime number whose digits added up to a prime number, like fifty-nine, where five plus nine is fourteen, which is not a prime number, but its digits (one and four) add up to five, which is prime, and therefore wholesome and righteous). If we failed in this, Gloria's crew would lose the Bike Stunt Trick Tournament.

Using a pen and paper (for calculators were forbidden) she tried to find a numerically safe path through these tiles. But the effort caused her eyes to bleed and brought Gloria to her knees, clutching her skull. She said, "It's like being stabbed in the brain by the sun."

Then Gloria McStepanovich saw the bug in the very middle of the labyrinth of cracks. It was a long bug with many legs, and it was so long that it wrapped around itself, and in fact was more like a tangled knot which writhed. It untangled and retangled itself in perpetuity.

Her bleeding eyes lit up and she said, "I see the path, for the the tiles light up like unto a video game, showing me which are numerologically safe," and she stepped upon them like an angel, carrying her dirtbike over one shoulder (with me on top), until she reached the bug.

She extended her free hand to the bug and it crawled onto her palm, and it seemed happy to finally be there. "It tickles my skin with its joyful wriggling." She did not put it into her mouth but instead put it next to her mouth and let it crawl inside. Then it crawled down her throat and she helped it with a swallow, and it became part of her. "I needed to wait for the bug to offer itself to me, which it had not done before. It had needed time to observe me and judge my worthiness."

Her eyes stopped bleeding and the highway became whole. We continued down the road with the fresh blessing in Gloria's belly.

Sammy McToby

by Abby Stanley

I'm an amateur dirtbike rider myself, and that's how I caught up to Sammy McToby on the highway. I asked if I could join him as a fly-on-the-wall reporter, but he shook his blond head in the wind and sped away. I followed him anyway. He pulled over at a gas station in a gravel clearing that had been hacked into the unforgiving thicket. He entered the convenience store with a jingle and said to the cashier, "Got any work?"

"N'ery a plum to pick me love," lamented the permed lady who sat behind the cash desk, wearing an apron, rocking on a wooden rocking chair, knitting a long red scarf.

Sammy said, "I'm not picky 'bout plums. I can clean tielets an' 'aul 'azardous waste. I got a university degree. Maybe yer boss got somethin' he needs done. May be legal, may be not. I got no limits. A man's gotta eat before a big dirtbike tournament."

"I don't work directly for the gas station," the lady told him. "I'm a contract worker. Now the man what owns the contracting comp'ny he's the same man what owns the gas station and he rents me out to hisself, takin' a small cut for the overhead. He's upstairs now."

The stairwell was pitch black and each step was a different depth, height, and angle. Sammy stumbled all the way up like a drunken madman and finally tumbled into the office where a bearded sailor sat behind a splintered desk wearing a yellow slicker and tuque of lapis lazuli, stamping a stamp onto stacks of paperwork.

"Got any work?" Sammy inquired.

"Argh ye bucky bastard place yer hand upon this desklike crucible and accept yer judgement."

Sammy placed his hand on the desk and the sailor stamped it hard, and the stamp was smoking hot and it burned a letter M onto the skin. "Now yer hired, me b'y."

"Okay, what feats shall I perform?"

"I got no feats needs performin' just yet, ye bucky little buckster. But I do got some featsters lookin' for feats to perform, and if they can find em then I gets a cut. Five dollars plus a percentage. So I wants you to head on down the road seekin' work for me contractors, eh me blubby?"

"So me job is to... go seek work?"

"And if ya finds it then I gets a cut."

Sammy fell down the stairs and got on his dirtbike and continued on down the road until he came to the next gas station, which was identical to the one we'd just departed. Inside he found the same lady who directed him up another darkened set of stairs. The depths and widths and angles of these steps was all different, so what he'd learned last time didn't help him from stumbling like an idiot up and into an identical office to the last, with an identical sailor stamping and stomping his stamps onto paperwork.

"Got any work?" Sammy asked, as if trapped in a dream.

"No me b'y, I've no such thing. And yet I suspect I can find ye something. Just place yer hand upon this desklike crucible and I'll gather ye into me service and set ye on the path to prosperity."

Sammy placed his other hand on the desk and the sailor burnt a W upon it and said, "Now head on down the road and solicit some work fer me b'ys. And I gets a cut. Five dollars plus a percentage."

Sammy got on his bike and kept riding until he found a time machine broken down on the side of the road. A man and a woman of numinous age tinkered with its innards. Sammy pulled over and said, "Got any work?"

The man said, "You arrived just in time. My name is Garth and this is my daughter Cecilia, who is also my wife and my mother. We have to repair our time machine and prevent this time-looped cycle of incest, though it means neither of us will ever be born (I'm also my own father)."

"Let's discuss terms," Sammy said.

"Our time machine has made us very rich via time-looped compound interest," Garth explained. "So I will pay you one billion dollars once we get this time machine up and running. Just hold this antenna like so."

Sammy held the antenna and the time machine

disappeared, and so did Garth and his wife and daughter and mother and father. All that was left was the empty road, and the trees so green hiding such darkness that crept into our hearts.

Unpaid he continued along this road at a forlorn pace until he came upon an identical gas station. I heard his engine putter as he ran out of gas and had to pull in. Up the stairs he went once more and asked the sailor, "I needs to borrow gas in advance outta me wages."

"Wages?" the sailor laughed. "Ye owes us infinite dollars already, me b'y. Me and meself, we rented ye out to each other in infinite regress, five dollars plus a percentage per iteration. Don't worry though. We ain't psychopaths. Simply work for us both forever without pay and we'll call it even. Ye'll find yer gas tank ne'er empty, and yer tummy always full, but all yer time belongs to us."

Sammy groaned and the Sailor said, "Is ya okay b'y?"

"Well me colon sure hurts," Sammy answered. "But neveryoumind that. What d'ya need me to do?"

"Me contracting company needs new recruits. Take

this here stamp, set forth and recruit, folding friend and foe into the cycle of prosperity, yea, unto the end of time."

Bobby Bardo

by Alice Appleton

I took the sneaky approach to bearing witness of Bobby Bardo's trek. I hid in the bushes and watched him pump his gas. Then I followed on my own dirtbike, a dirtbike built for ladies, and I watched him, and I felt like I could see inside his soul.

In the darkest hour of night we rode. His head jerked about and he looked here and there, like a hunted dog expecting a beating. The stars glistened like the eyes of cosmic spies. He was fidgety like a squirrel. I drove so close that I heard him whisper beneath the growl of our engines, "Those men could be anywhere with their truck. They could be hiding in the trees, or up around the next bend, or just over the horizon. If they catch me and put me in their truck then I'll never meet my five person crew for the tournament. I can't let them down."

A delightful twinkling noise emanated from the forest. And then a lower resonant tone. It was a piano, a beautiful piano, and Bobby Bardo seemed helpless to resist. He stopped his bike on the side of the road and moved his thick, beautiful hair away from his ear to better hear the piano sounds.

"Bhrams," he whispered. "Intermezzo in E minor, opus one one nine, number two. And it's being played by a woman."

Mesmerized by this siren song he walked down the embankment and into the thickness of the forest. He penetrated the impenetrable branches and pushed his way toward the source of the sound until he emerged into a clearing and saw a woman sitting at a grand piano. She had fair skin and black hair, a red dress covering a lean figure and she played with such passion that he fell to his knees. The moon shone above, smiling coldly. Bobby crawled to her and she turned her head without breaking sonic stride and said, "Stand, my love. I have brought you here."

He stood and approached the pianist. Placed his hands on her shoulders, and the straps of her dress became butterflies that flew away, and her dress melted away, and she was naked. He cupped one small breast in his hand and felt its weight, then put his lips in the soft valley of her neck, kissing her, and her beautiful notes sparkled like the stars.

She lay down on the bench, but her hands became detached and continued to play. She lay down and looked at him with smiling alien eyes, and he beheld her body and he kissed her from head to toe and back again. He made love to her handless body, and she wrapped her handless arms around him until he had spent himself gloriously within her.

Then he stood back and looked at her naked body. They floated atop the piano as her disembodied hands tickled the ivory. Her body writhed with joy, and she glistened with sweat and seed, and she said, "I am thirsty, my love. Fetch me a drink."

"I can smell the creek," he said. He followed the wholesome scent, and I followed him through the darkness of the forest, where we could not see the stars, and he knelt over the stream that burbled forth from the earth, and caught the water in his hands. He stood and turned to bring the water back to his lover, when headlights unconcealed themselves harshly within the forest. Men in ski masks grabbed him, but he couldn't defend himself without spilling the water. They shoved him in the back of the truck, and the truck drove away.

I followed the truck until it stopped and the men pulled Bobby out and they tied him to a stake that plunged into the ground, surrounded by firewood. He still held the water in his hands. The men still wore ski masks, and they were red ski masks, and their eyes were pure static. They must be off-duty cops.

"You've finally captured me," Bobby said. "Please tell me who sent ya."

"Who hasn't sent us?" asked the men. The four kidnappers paced around the pile of wood striking matches and tossing them in. Each match burnt out but I knew that eventually one would catch, and the water in Bobby's hands would boil away, his lover would remain thirsty, his bike crew would lose the tournament. His hands trembled and he said, "The prospect of letting down my team or my lady is what trembles my hands, not fear of burning, not even my aching spleen." But despite the trembling he never spilled a drop.

The kidnappers continued, "All the pianists who you made pregnant, they formed a union to extract your unpaid child support payments. They hired us to retrieve that payment."

"I got no money to pay em," he protested. "When the fisheries shut down I had n'erry a choice but to turn to dirtbike stunt trick tournaments, like thousands of other hard workin' Newfoundlanders. But it's a hard truck I tell ya."

The kidnapper-cops said, "You seduced them ladies and got em preggo, now you gotta pay up."

"But they seduced me," he protested. "And then they abandoned me. They used me for me seed then left me in a lurch. How d'ya figure to get child support payments from burnin' me alive, eh?"

"There's one kinda payment and then there's another," said the men. Then one of the matches caught a stray leaf, and a fire began.

At that very moment there was a great pianal upheaval. It was from Wagner's Fantasia in F-sharp minor and it came from everywhere. It came from the trees and the stars and the earth, even from the growing fire. The song lifted the static-eyed kidnappers up into the air where they kicked in confusion, and it brought them together, and it smushed them together into a bloody screaming mess, crushing their bones and spilling their guts to douse the flames, and a great glitchy static exploded from their ruined bodies and escaped into the wondrous night.

Then Bobby's piano playing lover flew in from the forest, still naked and glistening handlessly. She kissed him and she drank the water in his hands. She untied his bindings with her toes. He wept as they flew together over the horrifying darkness of the tangled conifer madness. The piano flew alongside them, played by her disembodied hands.

Something happened and now he was on his dirtbike, with her seated behind him wearing the red dress again, and her hands were attached to her wrists like a normal lady, and they were driving to meet his crew, and I was riding behind them on my ladybike, spying on their love.

Mike McFist

by James Lukeman

I was assigned to write this article about Mike McFist, the fifth member of the Home Team. But I refused to submit the article because I learned that Mike has a fetish for fascists, and he always carries a few around with him. He's also a sexual pervert (not that I would judge a man's predilections if they don't impose on another's, which his do). Suffice it to say that he encountered some protesters during his trek and he had an adventure but he didn't learn anything and I don't want to talk about it. Also he has a funny mole on his bald scalp.

Pre-Game Meet-Down

by Alton Abernathy

My fellow journalists joined me in Bikeminster on the day of the Bike Stunt Trick Tournament, though all had been changed by their journeys. The Home Team sat at a picnic table outside a coffee store, chewing coffee beans.

A wild doctor appeared with neat hair and a stethoscope. He looked at the Home Team (and Bobby's piano hottie) and said, "I have bad news. I just did a pre-game checkup on your enemy team, and they all got AIDS."

Mattias said, "All of em?"

"They're a polycule," the doctor explained. "Where one goes they all go. Even to AIDS."

Mike McFist looked up from his fascist pinup calendar and said, "This will be like stealing candy from a leper."

The doctor said, "Now it's time for your pre-game checkup." He put his stethoscope against Mister Mattias' mohawk and listened closely, and wrote something down on his fuckin' little notepad. He pressed a finger against Gloria McStepanovich's left eyeball and counted a few seconds on his watch, then scribbled more notes. He told Sammy McToby to stick out his tongue and then clunked the extended tongue with a little rubber hammer and inscribed another note. He grabbed Bobby Bardo's junk and listened to him yelp then wrote thoughtfully. Finally he gazed deep into Mike McFist's eyes and studied his soul, and ruefully wrote the longest note of all.

"I have bad news" the doctor said. "Mister Mattias, yer violent cough is a symptom o' Gloria's colon cancer. Gloria, yer headaches prove that Sammy's got esophageal cancer. Sammy, that pain in yer colon is from Bobby's ocular cancer. Bobby, yer achin' spleen is the final stages of Mike's brain cancer. And Mike, that mole on yer head is from Mister' Mattias' leukemia."

"The circle is complete," the bikesters said in unison.

"The only ting that could possibly save ya is medical experiments," the doctor told em.

Bike Stunt Trick Tournament

by Alton Abernathy

The town of Bikeminster was built around a meteor impact crater. When the meteor had hit, according to local geologists, it liquified the ground and caused molten ripples which quickly froze because it was such a cold day. Now the crater was a smooth bowl surrounded by ripples spreading outwards in rising concentric circles.

The very inner ripples were the perfect size for doing dirbike stunt tricks, and the outer circles served nicely as uncomfortaable seats for spectators. Dozens of Bikeminsterians gathered for today's Bike Stunt Trick Tournament. Our five heroes stood to one side, revvin' their bikes, and the enemy team stood across from them revvin' their own.

"They all looks the same," Sammy McToby said. Indeed, the enemy team all wore blue helmets and were indistinguishable. "They must be mainlanders."

"They's from Trana," Bobby Bardo said. "Lookit. Wherever they go there's the See Yen Tower."

Our five heroes beheld the cardboard cutout of the See Yen Tower which floated and wobbled just beyond the treeline, the guardian angel of all Trannoians.

The announcer was strapped to a quad copter and he flew around with his megaphone and said, "Blue team goes first!"

One of the Trannoians cranked his torque and blasted down into the crater, then up the other side, then flew up into the air and did the most spectacular and complex arrangements of twists and spins that anyone had ever seen. But halfway into his jump we saw him die of AIDS and he fell dead on the ground between two concentric ripples.

"Disqualified!" yelled the announcer. "Home team up next!"

Mike McFist tore down the dip and shot up the rim, somehow doing an even more complex and heart-breakingly beautiful series of spins, twists, and contortions. But halfway through his trick we watched in horror as he died of Sammy's colon cancer and fell dead like his enemy. His bike exploded and speckled the Trannoians' blue jackets with burning bits of metal in random patterns, and now the Trannoians were no longer identical. They were different from each other, marked by their unique burns.

"Disqualified!" yelled the announcer once more. "Funeral break!"

We were solemn for the double funeral. A shadow haunted us because we knew that we each have only so many tricks left before our own time comes.

Then the remaining bikesters mounted their machines and prepared for the next round. The announcer said, "The old order was bad luck," so he reversed the order, letting our heroic Home Team go first.

Mister Mattias did a layback spin and triple axel combo, landing gracefully with a bow. Everybody clapped because it was truly impressive, and because he didn't die.

The Trannoians sent their next combatant, and

halfway through his jump he removed his helmet, displaying his strong manly face, and he grew a soul because of the pain he'd suffered at losing his friend and the scars he'd accumulated from Mike's exploded bike.

The announcer said, "Point to the Trannoians for growin' a soul!"

The crowd clapped tepidly because they were biased toward the Home Team, but still pleased that the man had grown a soul.

Sammy McToby went next, and he did a half-grab quadruple backflip and landed it like a pro to great applause.

The Trannoians sent their next contender, who gave birth to a baby girl mid-jump, and landed the bike while nursing. The crowd cheered, and the Trannoians got another point.

Bobby Bardo said, "It ain't lookin' good, b'ys. We's down by two, and got to tie it up, then win in overtime."

So on his turn Bobby did a jump right over the Trannoians and grabbed one of em by the collar and put him in a camel clutch, broke his back, and then fucked his ass to make him humble, old country style. The man was subsequently too humble and his back too broken to do a good trick, so the point for this round went to the Home Team.

Finally it was Gloria McStepanovich's turn. She did her jump but I saw her take out a notepad midair to calculate how many flips to do. She scratched out seventeen, a nice prime number, but scribbled that its digits were one and seven, which makes eight, which ain't prime. Michael Tuck (her biographer) told me how Gloria never trusted the number eight. It's just four twos in a trench coat, or maybe two fours in a rain slicker. She found an evil aspect to every number she considered. So she just stayed in the air spinning until the announcer disqualified her for staying in the air too long. He'd stopped her at flip number eighty-three. Tuck said, "At least it's prime, but the presence of that eight will haunt her."

The Trannoians had won. The two teams lined up for the handshake. As Sammy McToby shook each Trannoian hand he stamped them with the stamp from his recursive sailor boss. Then the announcer led the victors into the forest for their medical experiments.

The audience departed. The Home Team grew tired from their various cancers and gathered in the middle of the impact crater. It was nearly time to die. Bobby Bardo's piano hottie played a sad tune on her piano. She detached her hands and lay down and let Bobby make love to her one last time. The others watched, and it wasn't perverted, it was beautiful because they knew she was preggo now.

It wasn't so bad to lose, but it was always sad to die. But then they died, and the pianist shed a tear and closed their eyes with her toes. And she sat at her piano and flew into the forest, and the dirtbikes followed with her, doing tricks and stunts.

Werner Herzog in Space

Ray Diess coined the term "Herzogsploitation" for this piece. I published this on Substack, and previously on an old blog. The inclusion of a certain pre-insanity celebrity-inventor-businessman might not have aged well, but the overall story has.

The old filmmaker watched from the terrace as a shadow flitted across his darkened back lawn and disappeared through the white-stone archway below. Werner transferred the Beretta from his boot to his belt and went to confront this visitor who shunned the front door and the light.

The man ascending the stairs wore a gray woolen robe, his face hidden deep within his hood. Werner transferred the pistol from his belt to his palm, and transferred the safety to off.

The stranger reached into a pouch slung over his shoulder. Werner aimed the pistol at the shadowed face. "Show yourself," he directed, his voice leathery and uncompromising, accustomed to addressing the darkness and calling forth its secrets.

The visitor raised his hood and uncovered the visage of Elon Musk, a face full of childlike wonder and alien cunning. From his pouch he produced a model aeroplane with an unfamiliar teardrop design. Elon reached the top of the stairs and looked at the wall.

"You scoundrel," Werner said with a relieved chuckle, his Bavarian accent conveying warmth as easily as it had just conveyed death. He turned on the safety once more and lowered the pistol. "Why are you sneaking around? I almost shot you."

"Maybe you still will," the inventor-oligarch quipped. "I have bad news and the messenger always gets shot. Jeff Bezos is sending Michael Bay to Saturn to film a Superbowl commercial, with Coldplay accompanying him to provide the music."

"Excellent," Werner said. "Good riddance. Nobody can survive such a journey. Maybe they will cannibalize each other."

Elon added, "They also plan to build an interplanetary movie studio system specifically for super-hero movies."

Werner aimed the pistol between Elon's eyes and squeezed the trigger, but the safety was on. Scowling, he shoved the weapon back in his pants and walked over to his keg to pour two beers. "This is unacceptable. We must sabotage them. We must use all of our cunning."

Elon drank from the stout he was handed, thick as mud. "I have prepared something much better than sabotage."

"Of course you have. Tell me."

Elon handed the model plane to Werner. It was shaped like a teardrop with wings. The big front window revealed the cockpit. A tiny figure sat at the tiny console, with a face identical to Werner's own, with his serious sparkling eyes.

"If you leave tonight you can beat them," Elon said. "They plan to stop at Mars and visit several Jovian moons before reaching Saturn's orbit. You must be the first film director to document our solar system. This ship uses a top-secret propulsion system and answers only to a Bavarian accent. But I must warn you, because of fuel constraints it's a one-way trip."

"There are no other kinds. I shall name this ship The Heraclitus."

"Jeff Bezos will be super pissed when he finds out we've beaten him."

"Bezos is a bozo. He makes one web page and he

thinks he can conquer the solar system. I don't think so. But who will make the soundtrack? I doubt we can rouse Ernst at this hour."

"We tried to convince Trent Reznor to accompany you, but he declined. So we kidnapped him."

Elon put his fingers in his mouth and let loose a bird call. Soon two more figures ascended the staircase: a pale elf-woman hauling a man, and he was bound in leather from head to foot. She tugged on his chain and he dropped to his knees before the director. Then she unzipped his eyes-holes.

Werner put the model plane beneath Trent Reznor's chin and lifted it up to look in the slave's eyes. "He's washed up. I was hoping for Hootie and the Blowfish, but I suppose this will do. I have no quarrel with Coldplay but I cannot allow Michael Bay to do to Saturn's moons what he did to The Transformers."

"There's no time to waste," Elon urged. "Press the button on the bottom of the model to summon the ship."

Werner pressed the button. Within moments a light hum grew into an undulating thrum. A much larger version of the vessel landed on the back lawn. A team of engineers appeared out of the darkness with stencils and spray-paint to inscribe the words, "The Heraclitus" onto the shimmering blue hull, quick as a pit-crew, then disappeared once more.

"The ship is equipped with the best audio and video recorders," Elon explained, "as well as a wide variety of synthesizers and effects for Trent. There's enough food to get you to Saturn."

"I have one request before I leave this world," Werner told the billionaire. "Once I'm gone, go into my basement and destroy what you discover there. Do not ask questions and tell nobody what you see."

Elon's brows rose in intrigue, but he offered a pert nod. "Of course."

Then Werner took up Trent's chain. "Come slave," he said, and together they descended the stairs. Elon and his elf-queen watched from the terrace as the filmmaker and the musician entered the sleek craft. Then it lifted into the air.

In the cockpit Werner was surrounded by video

screens showing a full 360 degrees outside. In the back Trent fiddled with knobs on a rack of analog synths and effects.

Werner turned on the audio and video recorders, which also transmitted their feed to an earth-based server.

As they ascended Trent Reznor played one long note, starting as a simple tone which slowly built into a haunting chord, and beyond this into a triumphant cacophony of distorted reverb.

Werner narrated:

> *The Earth disappears below me. The acceleration is surprisingly mild as it pushes me down in my chair like a comforting hug. The engines are running smoothly.*
>
> *The lights of American cities sparkle far below, growing smaller and smaller as I join the stars above. I thought I would feel a sense of loss but instead I feel giddy like an escaping convict,*

but also nervous that my jailers might recapture me.

My control panel informs me that we have escaped the Earth's orbit. Now that I can see my planet in its entirety I can tell it what I really think. Earth, you are a carnival of horrors. Your children are all monsters and I loathe their cruelty. And yet, I miss my friends.

Reznor's chord dropped to a tragic key and went silent. He mumbled into the sound system, "Herr director, we have a bogey."

Werner sighed. "I can read my own screen, slave, thank you."

The radar showed a red dot approaching them at a dangerous speed, but not on a collision course. Werner cycled through the craft's many cameras until he caught a blurry image of the object pursuing them. It was a flying saucer with a steel brim and a glass dome. Through the transparent dome he could barely discern the stony visage of Michael Bay at the controls and Coldplay jamming behind him.

"They will overtake us and beat us to Mars," Werner lamented. "Their spacecraft is superior to our own."

"This machine is obsolete," Trent said, wiring up more synths and effects on the rack.

"You are not here to offer lyrical redundancies," Werner scolded his servant. "We need to torpedo them before they overtake us. But we brought no torpedoes. We must launch you at their flying saucer and hope your body slows them down."

"Too late," Trent Reznor said. "They've already launched their torpedoes at us."

The cameras showed a volley of MTV Movie Awards flying on an intercept course. "Evasive maneuvers," Werner said, punching controls to change the vessel's trajectory. They missed the bulk of the volley and several of the awards passed the vessel to join the stars. But one *Best Action Sequence Award for Armageddon (1998)* hit The Heraclitus' fin and sent it spinning out of control as Bay's shimmering saucer blasted past them in the blink of an eye. Werner caught a quick glimpse of Bay's smiling face, but Coldplay was giving him the finger. Then they were gone and *The Heraclitus* corkscrewed madly, its spin too chaotic for the ship's systems to autocorrect. Blinking lights and blazing sirens filled the cockpit.

Werner found himself too dizzy to work the controls. The stars spun past so fast he felt like vomiting. "It cannot end this way," he said. The ship's spin was still accelerating. "I cannot be defeated by the accolades of philistines. Yet I have always known this would be my fate."

The spin was so fast that the director was losing consciousness. But he saw Trent Reznor, chained to his synth rack, tearing open the ship's walls and rerouting wires and circuitry between the ship's systems and his electronic instruments.

"I think I can correct the spin with a low frequency oscillator," the audio engineer explained. His iron-hard muscles struggled against the centrifugal force. He bit the wires to strip off their casings and twisted the metal together, then slowly tweaked knobs on the effect pedals until the spin diminished. The stars rotated slower and slower until they finally stopped. Stabilized, the ship's autopilot corrected their trajectory so they were aimed at Mars again. But Michael Bay's flying saucer was nowhere to be seen.

"We survived," Herzog said joylessly, "but now we will never catch up to them. We live only to witness our own defeat."

"Maybe not," Reznor countered mildly. His chains clinked and rattled as he connected the ship and his sound system in an ever-deepening electronic symbiosis. The acceleration increased dramatically. Within seconds Werner saw the flying saucer in his screen. Soon they would be passing them.

"We must have vengeance," Werner intoned. "What can we launch at them? I need you alive now to operate the ship. I may have to launch myself."

"I have just the thing," the musician said with the slightest smile, tearing open yet another panel in the wall. "I'm taking control of our radio transmitter. We'll show these hacks the true power of music."

He turned up the reverb, distortion, and feedback, then hit a dissonant chord on his midi controller. It made no sound in *The Heraclitus*, but on his video screen Werner could see that their rivals' saucer had received the radio signal. They all clamped their palms over their ears and opened their mouths to scream uselessly. As *The Heraclitus* whizzed past the saucer, Chris Martin's head exploded like a pumpkin, splattering brains and blood over his horrified shipmates.

Werner laughed in triumph. "Now they know who they are dealing with. They will think twice before attacking me with their phony awards. Even if they defeat us in the end, we have given mister Bay the most exciting sequence of all his films. Thank you mister Reznor. You have saved my life and my dignity. I will remove your chains."

"No," Trent responded. "They make me happy."

Werner studied his slave with cheerful curiosity, "Very well. Now, I am an old man and I must nap. Wake me when we reach Mars."

Much later, Werner narrated:

I have never seen anything so un-wholesome as the landscape of Mars. It is horrifying to know that these planets exist. These empty worlds hold no life and no dreams, only violence and endless cold silence. I see rocks strewn across a rolling landscape of sand, and I wonder what stupid forces placed them there. A poison wind stirs up the dirt, and the worthlessness of this dirt is repeated all the way to the planet's barren core. This has been going on for billions of years, on billions of planets that nobody cares about. I only wish Kinski was still with us, so I could abandon him here. He might give this world some personality.

Trent Reznor played a long subtle chord as *The Heraclitus* glided over the Martian landscape at a low altitude of thirty meters. A slow-rising smooth volcano sloped up ahead of them on the horizon.

Werner's narration continued:

Occasional volcanoes tease us with evidence that something interesting might once have occurred on this corpse. Lava once flowed, back when Mars was young and still had potential. But now that potential is gone and in its place is the same cold stupidity that lies at the center of the human heart. This is our destiny. This is our god.

I keep hoping I might see some sign of life. Some madman who came out here to get away from the banality of civilization. I want to see what would happen to his mind. What kinds of ideas would infect his psyche? Would he remember how to speak? I envy the blissful silence of his mind. But I think he would just disappear, snap out of existence, for nothing could ever survive here.

I cannot even see this planet's pathetic moons

through the fog of dirt. I have already lost interest. Let's move on to another empty world.

The asteroid belt between Mars and Jupiter is a disappointment. I had hoped for more danger, dodging between a chaos of tumbling space-rocks, but the asteroids are far apart and easy to avoid. I suppose there is some majesty to their lonely vigilance. They do not know that nobody needs them, like soldiers in remote camps who don't know the war has been over for years. They exist despite our need for purpose. When they outlive us they will derive no joy from their victory.

Jupiter overwhelms my powers of de-scription. I will let my cameras do their work but even they cannot convey the majesty and horror of this god. One day our robotic descendants might drink the storms that cover her surface, and I dread what they will uncover below.

Trent Reznor interrupted his narration. "I'm receiving a signal from the surface of Io. I think it's Michael Bay. They must have passed us while we visited Mars."

An image appeared on one of the screens. Michael Bay stood within the dome of his spacecraft, eyes wild, his mouth covered in blood dripping down his chin and neck. He had cannibalized Coldplay and their chewed-up corpses surrounded him like a sacred mandala. Behind him, through the glass of the dome, Werner could see the landscape of the Jovian moon Io. Molten sulfur poured poisonous orange through fissures in the rocks at the base of an imposing mountain of shattered yellow and black stone. Above it all green and black clouds flashed with neon pink lightning.

Trent Reznor said, "The isolation of space, combined with Chris Martin's head exploding, must have pushed him over the edge."

Bay opened a comms link and said, "I found the base of The Transformers. They're inside the mountain. I have to go meet them."

"You've found no such thing," Werner transmitted back. "I beg you to stay inside your ship until we can retrieve you."

But Bay was already donning his space suit. "Only Optimus Prime under-stands me."

"If you must go then bring your camera, you doomed fool."

"I'll get an Oscar for this for sure."

Werner watched Michael Bay's final moments as the director of *Pain & Gain (2013)* entered into the opening in the rocks and was consumed by the sickly sulfur boiling out from the moon's innards. Then Werner deleted that portion of the video, recording only his commentary. "Nobody must ever watch this. Know only that this man transformed himself into a quixotic angel. He wished only to entertain. He brought himself to the limit and then stepped beyond. If only I could be so bold."

Silence followed. Then Trent Reznor began to play a tragic homage to the late director of *Bad Boys II (2003)*.

"I suppose I should move on to Saturn," Werner said, though his heart wasn't in it. He felt he should mourn longer for Michael Bay, but their food supplies were dwindling.

"We don't have the fuel to escape Jupiter's orbit," Trent explained. "We spent too much correcting our spin after the MTV Movie Awards attack."

Werner grinned sadly. "The people have spoken. We will leave it for the next generation to probe the outer solar system. For now *The Heraclitus* will follow in the footsteps of the great Galileo. No stone will mark our graves, but when Earth receives our video transmission it will leave a mark upon their souls. They will see that space offers only doom, and they will be compelled to confront and conquer it.

> *Behold the clouds that consume me. They swirl and they dance. They have been waiting for us. They cannot reject me now. Let me in, you faeries! You gods! Though I will not survive you, I will die among you. This is my final cut. But for my species let this be the end of the opening act.*

LARRY GRANK VS THE FLAT EARTH

Today you will finally learn the truth.

Gary was squinting through his binoculars. "I think I see Antarctica," he said. His breath puffed out as a cloud of condensed desperation.

"Not for another two days," I reminded him. But I still nervously peered at the cold waters of the horizon, worried he might be right.

"These binoculars compensate for refraction," he explained.

"They can't compensate for the horizon," I countered.

"There's no horizon on an endless plane."

We were on the deck of the *Ice Blecher*, a research vessel headed to the northernmost continent of our spheroid planet. Gary was an avid reader of my newsletter and had hired me to document his journey. He intended to prove that the Earth was flat, and that Antarctica was really the gateway to endless fantastic lands, including the kingdoms that truly controlled our world. Gary had been brainwashed by blogs and online videos, and the fool thought that I'd be sucked in to the same lies.

Gary thrust the binoculars at me. "Just look. With these refraction-correcting binoculars you can see Antarctica."

"I see something," I admitted. "But I think it's another boat, or maybe some garbage."

"I think it's a continent. And if we trek across that continent we'll find out who's really running the show. And you can write that in your newsletter."

"Oh I'll document the whole journey in my newsletter," I assured him. "But after we hire a black-market sherpa what we'll find is secret CIA laboratories." My sources had given me solid evidence that the bleeding edge of human cloning and sex-majick was being developed on that remote continent.

"Actually it does look like garbage," Gary finally admitted after I gave the binoculars back. "But I think I see Antarctica behind the garbage."

It turned out to be a shipwreck. Three men were clinging to the remnants of their crashed ship.

"This is bait," I told Gary. "Don't pick these men up.

They're government spies and they're onto us. They know we're going to discover their genetic research labs."

"Let's just hear what they have to say," Gary rejoined. He didn't like me bossing him around. My superior intellect gave him small-man syndrome.

Aside from Gary and me there were four other men on the *Ice Blecher*. Pete was the janitor, another man named Pete was the cook, and two men whose names were Fritz piloted the boat in shifts.

"Fritz!" Gary yelled. "Bring us up to the shipwreck!"

Fritz did as he was asked, and soon we pulled to a stop among a wasteland of wooden slabs and crates bobbing in the ice-cold waves.

Gary pointed down at the survivors and asked, "What happened to your ship?"

"An iceberg smashed us!" one of them yelled back. "Asteroids of the sea!"

"Lies," I whispered in Gary's ear. "It's too convenient. The government knows that I'm about to discover their CIA labs on Antarctica, and they sent these men to intercept us. They're the enemies of truth. You can't trust them."

Gary pondered this. He looked longingly at the horizon. "Is the Earth flat?" he asked the freezing strangers. "Or is it round?"

"We just came from Antarctica!" one of them yelled back. "We met the Transcendental Emperor who occludes the infinity of Earth, he showed us the Flat Secrets of our Planet!"

"You have proof?" Gary demanded.

One of the men gestured to the large crates bobbing in the water. "Crates and crates of proof! Just haul us in, please!"

I turned to Fritz and said, "Fritz, you don't believe these guys, do you? You've been a sea man since you were a boy, you must know the Earth is round, and that these are government spies."

"Don't care is she's round or flat," Fritz said, "long as she's wet!"

Gary's hired crew had consistently refused to weigh in on our ongoing argument. I respected their resolve.

I'm very persuasive and my logic is diamond-sharp. But sailors are hard men.

Soon the crew were hauling men and crates up onto the deck. Somebody lit a barrel fire and we all sat around roasting salt pork and cod as the sun set. They introduced themselves as Werner, Warner, and Warwick.

Gary rudely pointed at me and said to the newcomers, "My friend Larry thinks the planet is round, he believes the government lies."

Werner said, "There's a reason it's called a planet and not a curvet or a roundet."

I refused to argue with the spies so I turned my dialectical inquiry to Gary. "I know UFOs are real because the government officially admits that they're real. You see, no intelligent person trusts the government, but the government knows that, so they tell the truth to make intelligent people believe that it's false. But they pay spies like these guys to unofficially spread flat-earth lies so that we'll stop paying attention to their alliances with aliens from planets that you don't even believe exist."

"Other planets exist, but they're flat too. You're paranoid."

"And you're a credulous fool. You'll see that I'm right when we find the genetic research labs on the finite continent of Antarctica. They have to do their research there because of the human rights violations. They're speeding up evolution, churning out freaks and killing most of them off in an effort to create the ultimate race of super soldiers, or docile worker drones."

"We won't have to wait," Gary said. He turned to our guests. "Let's open those crates and show Larry your proof!"

"Time enough for that once we get warm and eat some cod," said Warwick, their captain. He had a thick beard and serene black eyes. Their crates were stacked behind us.

I heard a knocking sound and a mournful wail.

"Did you hear that mournful wail?" I asked.

"Probably a mournful whale," Werner said dismissively as he munched on some cod.

"What about that knocking sound?" I pressed. "It sounds like it's coming from your crates."

"That's just our evidence," Warner answered. "Our proof of the Earth's flatness."

I grabbed a nearby crowbar. "Let's open the fucker up and take a look inside."

The three rescuees stood up. "Time enough for that in the morning. We're super tired after a hard day of being shipwrecked."

"Pete, show these fine men to their bunks," Gary said. He was totally in their thrall. I was embarrassed by his lack of suspicion. I looked like a fool for being associated with him.

I descended into the bowels of the research vessel, toward my bunk. The ship creaked and groaned, gently rocking with the waves as Fritz nocturnally navigated up above. Shadows danced across the walls and in my heightened awareness my mind perceived enemies lurking in their murky depths. But I arrived at my room unmolested.

I locked the door twice, once with its built-in sliding

lock and again with a padlock attached to a chain that I'd welded on. There were no police out on the open sea, but there were other enemies.

I couldn't sleep. I tossed and turned on the hard cot. What was keeping me awake? I searched my thoughts and decided it must be our three new passengers. But what specifically about them had me so worried? They had appeared on our path much too conveniently. I feared they were spies sent by the CIA to prevent me from reaching Antarctica, where I would surely discover their black-ops genetic-engineering compounds. Yes, I feared they were sent to sabotage my mission.

But I also feared the opposite. A nagging worry tickled the bottom of my mind like a feather of dreadful possibility. Maybe, just maybe, they really had proof that the Earth was flat. What was in those boxes? I was frightened and intrigued. Frightened at the possibility that my whole worldview was wrong, intrigued and excited at the prospect of a whole new worldview to explore.

But of course that's exactly what they wanted me to

feel. They had withheld the crucial information, teasing me with mystery. They wanted me to speculate, to wonder, to be propelled into a fantasy of their design by my unquenched curiosity!

But then, what was really in those crates? What had we invited into our midst?

In the creaking of the lonesome ship I heard a voice. "Larry," it whispered. "They have infiltrated us, Larry, and you're the only one we can trust!"

"Who is that?" I whispered back, sitting up in my bed.

"They want to hurt us, Larry! You have to stop them."

Shadows played in the corners of my room. The slightest light from my charging cell phone cast dancing figures on my periphery, but when I looked they were gone.

"Who are you?" I insisted. "Are you a ghost? A faerie? Are you the ship itself?"

"We are the ghosts of research expeditions past, poisoned by our own experiments, drowned in the ocean, stung by manta rays. The only things that unite us are our love of knowledge and our unfinished research. We sense that you're a kindred spirit searching for truth. But the interlopers, Larry, they are the enemies of truth. They've come to stop you from uncovering knowledge. They're attacking the ship even as we speak. If you don't stop them you'll never reach Antarctica, and this ship will never be used for research ever again!"

"I knew it!" I exclaimed. I hopped out of bed and put on some trousers and a shirt. "Where are they? How can I stop them?"

"You must go to the engine room, Larry. They're poisoning our engine!"

I grabbed a flashlight, unlocked my padlock, and slid open the sliding lock. When I swung the door open I saw Werner standing in the doorway wearing pyjamas.

"I can't sleep," he said. "I think I heard a ghost. Can I sleep in your room?"

"There's no such thing as ghosts," I lied. "Now go back to bed!"

But then a breeze whispered through the hall, carrying that same ghostly voice which said, "No Larry! Don't send him to bed! He's a spy! You must neutralize him!"

"There!" Werner cried. "You hear it?"

"Hear what?" I asked, and bashed him over the head with my flashlight. The cheap plastic light broke into a dozen pieces. Werner tried to run but I grabbed the elastic of his pyjama pants and yanked them down so he tripped and fell. I used my phone's charging cord to bind his hands and asked the ghost, "Should I throw him overboard?"

"No!" the ghost responded. "We need him for our research. For our experiments."

"What kind of experiments?" I asked. Ghosts and scientists are known for their ambivalence to, or even penchant for, human misery.

"You have to break a few eggs to invent new kinds of omelettes," the voice responded in a sinister tone. "Are you dedicated to truth and knowledge, Larry? Or are you one of them?"

I was indeed dedicated to truth and knowledge. So I tied Werner up to my bed.

"Now stuff a sock in his mouth to keep him quiet and

put a pillowcase over his head," the voice instructed. "It's a sensory deprivation experiment!"

I followed the instructions and ventured out into the hall to find the engine room.

It wasn't a big ship but somehow at night the halls became a labyrinth. I lost my way almost immediately and had to trust the voice to lead me to my destination. "Turn left, Larry. Now right! Yes, through this door! Yes! You're getting closer!"

When I finally found the engine room it had already been infiltrated. Warner was there, opening a valve on a pipe, draining black fluid into a bucket. His back was turned and he didn't hear me enter, because I was wearing sneakers and consider myself well trained in stealthcraft.

"He is draining our precious fluids, Larry," the ghost lamented in a strained, victimized voice. "You must stop him, Larry!"

"What's that noise?" Werner asked, turning around, looking for the source of the faint voice. He spotted me and I pounced. We wrestled on the ground. He pulled my hair and I elbowed his neck. He was stronger than me and he would have won, but I grabbed a thick handful of the black fluid from his bucket and splashed it on his face and into his mouth, causing him to reel back, choking and gagging.

"There's a rope in the corner, Larry," the ghost-voice informed me. "Use it. Tie him up."

I did as I was asked. Then I said, "Should I fix this pipe?"

"Not yet, Larry. It's time for our first experiment. Do you see the first aid kit on the wall?"

I retrieved the kit.

"Yes, Larry. Do you see the IV needle and tubes? Beneath the gauze and antiseptic? Yes. Take them out, Larry. Connect the tube to the spout on the pipe that Warner was draining."

I found the spout and attached one end of the plastic tube to its mouth. "Now what?" I asked the voice.

"Attach the needle to the end of the tube, and put the needle in Warner's arm, Larry."

"Why?"

"It's an experiment, Larry. This is a precious fluid. A magical fluid. This is how we acquire knowledge, Larry."

I jammed the needle into Warner's arm and the black fluid rushed into his veins.

"What are you doing to me?" Warner asked in fright.

I answered his question with a question. "Why were you draining the ship's precious fluids?"

He shook his head. "You don't know what you're doing. This ship... it's evil!"

I grabbed his shoulders and shook him. "Who are you? What are you doing on our ship?"

But his eyes rolled back in his head and he fell over on the floor.

"His transformation has begun," the voice told me. "But our experiments will never be safe until you catch Warwick, too."

I already knew where I could find Warwick. He would be up on the deck, with those crates full of evidence of the flat Earth.

As I crept up the stairs the ghost voice started humming an Aleksandr Scriabin tune. It really put me in the right mood for research and science. The rhythm of the music matched the ship's ocean-borne sway. I reached the deck and saw that the waves had grown stronger in the night's dark. Foamy peaks lashed the air. The crates sat where they had been stacked, imposing cubic shadows.

"Hello Larry," a voice boomed. I looked up and saw Warwick standing atop the nearest crate. He had been holding a harpoon and threw it like a spear before I had a chance to dodge. It completely impaled my shoulder and pinned me to the deck.

The pain wasn't as bad as the fear. Warwick jumped down and stood over me. Lightning flashed in the sky, illuminating the craziness of his beard. "So you thought you could uncover the truth, did you?"

"Who are you?" I demanded. But I wasn't in a position to make demands, pinned like a beautiful butterfly.

"I am the keeper of truth, Larry. And you are my enemy. With your critical thinking skills and lust for knowledge, I can't allow you to live."

A knife appeared in his hand. It looked like I was finished. But in the next flash of lightning I saw Gary emerge in the doorway, and in the next flash I saw him raising a seal-bashing club. He rushed Warwick and clobbered him over the head. Warwick stumbled, reeling toward the rail. Pete and Fritz appeared on either side of him, grabbing his arms.

"Should we throw him overboard?" they asked.

"Not yet," Gary said. He approached the murderous coveter of truth. "Warwick, tell me now, is the Earth round or is it flat?"

"Why don' t you ask this cursed ship?" he roared, spittle flying from his lips.

The other Fritz reached into Warwick's pocket and pulled out a wallet, then pawed through its contents. "He works for the CIA!"

"I knew it!" I called out. "He's been playing you the whole time! He just wants to protect the CIA's secret genetic laboratories!"

"You're asking all the wrong questions," Warwick boomed. Then he threw off his captors and leapt into the ocean.

Pete came and removed the harpoon, then Pete cleaned and bandaged my wound. "This will leave a cool scar," he commented.

"But what's in these boxes?" Gary mused. Something inside was still knocking. "Let's crack them open."

Pete and Fritz got some crowbars and got to work trying to open the boxes.

Then the ghost voice whispered in my ear, "We need more people for our experiments, Larry. Fritz and Pete and Gary would be perfect. You have to capture them, Larry. Capture them with the fishing net."

"But they helped me," I argued. "They're my friends."

"Pete and Fritz don't care about the truth," the voice reminded me. "They wouldn't even defend you against Gary when he argued that the Earth was flat. And Gary... don't even get us started on Gary."

I knew that the voice was right, though it hurt my heart to admit it. Experimentation was one of the best paths to truth, and experiments needed subjects. Subjects like these enemies of truth. So while my shipmates were cracking open the crates I snuck up behind them with the net, and cast it over them like a school of fish.

"What's this?" they cried, but it was too late. They were tangled and helpless. I tied them up and brought them below, while they protested my treachery.

When the sun came up the sea was calm once more. I had the whole ship to myself. Just me and the ghosts, doing human experiments on the high seas.

"It's time to open the crates, Larry," the ghosts told me. "It's time to learn the truth."

I gleefully cracked open the crates. Inside each one I found a dozen adult humans, curled up and sleeping in their own stinking filth. And each one looked exactly like me.

"Clones?" I asked. "Clones of myself?"

"That's right, Larry," the ghosts said. "And they can help us with our experiments."

"Do they have my memories?"

"No, you can't clone memories Larry, that's not how cloning works."

"Well then they're not really me," I said, disappointed.

"We can train them. Consider it a social experiment."

"I guess so."

"Cheer up, Larry. You're a captain now. A captain of Truth, with a crew of clones, and people to do experiments on. It's all a man could ever wish for."

And in the dawn's early light I finally appreciated the gift that had been given to me. The gift of knowledge, and the responsibility of searching for truth. I was bound to the ship like Prometheus was bound to his rock. And I rode that ship where the voices instructed, for they were the voice of truth, and I their humble servant.

Haunted Chocolate

I originally published this story in a collection called *The Paranoid Adventures of Larry Grank* in 2014. It's slightly sillier than the others, but also heart-warming and full of wisdom.

I reached for my chocolate gnome, but he wasn't there. Swivelling around on my chair I scanned my bachelor apartment and saw him sitting on a distant stool instead of the desk where I'd put him.

"Helloo, Larroo," the gnome said to me from inside his cardboard box, smiling through the thin plastic window.

I frowned. "My name's not Larroo, it's Larry. Plus how did you get over there?"

"Hellaa, Larraa," the gnome teased me. It bugged me how he said my name wrong. "Hollee, Larrow."

I walked to the stool, reaching out for the Belgian delight. As my fingers closed on the prize, the box disappeared.

"Hellaa Larraa," said a voice behind me. I turned and the gnome was sitting on my swivel chair. I could almost taste him melting in my mouth, but he was magically elusive. Why was this happening? It must be revenge from a magician who I've angered. There are many.

"What do you want from me?" I asked.

"Herroo, Lally!"

I lunged for the chocolate, crumpling the box in both hands and shaking with the laughter of victory. "I caught you!"

"Helliie, Larrow." The gnome was back across the room sitting on the stool. The crumpled box in my hands was empty.

"I'll turn up the heat, and then you'll melt," I snarled seriously, like an action hero. Then I noticed a phone number written on the box. It said, *Is there something wrong with your chocolate gnome? Call this number.*

So I locked the door and took out my cell phone. The number rang once and a jolly man answered with his smooth Arabian accent, saying, "Greetings, chocolate lover! For what do I owe the great pleasure of your call?"

"My chocolate gnome is haunted," I told him. "He keeps disappearing across the room and mispronouncing my name."

"Sir, a grievous wrong has been done to your family and your empire if this gnome is mispronouncing your name due to some evil enchantment. Can you stimulate the beast into performing his ill deeds while I listen? See if he will mispronounce your name again."

I held the cell phone out at the gnome. "Say something!"

The gnome smiled at me, and he was so chocolatey that I just couldn't hate him. Still, I grabbed my stapler from the desk and threw it at him. He disappeared just as the stapler whizzed through his space. Then he reappeared on the top shelf of my closet. "Hellaa, Larroo!"

"There, did you hear him?"

"Oh yes," said the telephone. "Your chocolate is surely haunted, which is such a shame since those gnomes are so very delicious. Tell me, where did you buy this treat?"

"A little chocolate shop in Kensington Market," I said. "It seemed harmless and mundane."

"Little in this world is as it seems," the jolly man said, suddenly serious.

"I almost bought chocolate-covered ants instead," I said. "Now I wish I had."

"I would tell you to abandon this chocolate gnome

and find some other place to buy your dessert from now on, except it is too late for that. I would tell you to burn this chocolate and let the flames eat up all the evil, but I am afraid it is not that simple. More work will be required of you before your empire is safe once more."

"My empire is only a bachelor apartment," I said, "but it's full of important secrets."

"I'm sure it is," said the man. "Now let us work together to keep it safe. You must have the chocolate de-haunted, and then you must feed it to a maiden so that evil cannot penetrate the material again."

"Does it have to be a human maiden?" I asked, looking at my sleeping cat.

"Of course. But first, the de-haunting. I will give you an address and a name, and you will visit this man."

I said, "How can I take the chocolate with me? He keeps disappearing."

"The gnome will follow you. This is part of the curse."

I wrote down the name and address.

I exited my apartment, leaving the chocolate gnome behind. I couldn't wait to dehaunt him and eat him.

When I reached the stairs, the gnome was sitting on the floor of the lower landing. He said, "Ah, halla, Larraaa! Helloo Larroo!"

I waded through the crowded streets. Everybody else was engaged in work or leisure, but I had a paranormal mission. None of them could comprehend the otherworldly weight of my task. My life is much more serious than theirs. "Halla Loorrooo!" I looked around and saw him on the canopy above a fruit stand. Then he disappeared.

The address led me into the Arabian district. Bluejeans and hoodies were replaced by robes and turbans, the smells of weed and car exhaust were replaced by rich spices, and pavement replaced with sand. I twisted through side-streets and alleys, following Google Maps on my phone. Everybody looked like an assassin because their faces were covered against the sandy wind. The chocolate appeared on a balcony, in a baby's cradle, and finally in a window above the entrance to my destination. "Hellee Leerree!" He cried as I knocked on the wooden door.

The door swung immediately open, revealing a tunnel-like stone hallway. A dusty red carpet ran deep into the building and torches hung on the wall. One robed figure stood before me with eyes glowing red. "I have a haunted chocolate gnome," I said.

The figure nodded.

"Are you Marcel the Dehaunter?"

The figure nodded again, backing away from the door and gesturing me inside with a bow. He seemed to hover smoothly over the ground instead of walking. I said, "Magic man, this haunted chocolate is poor business practice, unprofessional conduct, and-"

I felt a cold finger press against my lips, and those red eyes gazed into mine. "I do not haunt chocolates!" Marcel snapped at me in a sharp, indiscernible accent. "I am the de-haunter, and you must thank me instead of lecturing me."

"I'll thank you after I'm eating that chocolate," I said. He floated backwards away from me and I followed him deeper into his den.

He waved a finger at me. "You must never eat the

chocolate," he said. "When it is de-haunted you must feed it to a maiden, or else the ghost will find its old host within your tummy. This we cannot allow."

"Well what's the point in dehaunting him at all, then? I should just leave the chocolate here."

"He will follow you forever."

"Helloo Larroo!" The voice came from behind me, and I could barely see his little silhouette on the floor.

Marcel said, "The chocolatiers, they will reimburse you with more chocolate. You will be given two chocolate gnomes instead of one. Pure chocolate, untainted by evil."

"I just want my money back," I said.

"This they will not do," Marcel said. "Many have tried."

We came to a great circular room with a round stone table in the centre. The table had a pentagram drawn on it with chalk, and a red candle burned and melted upon each of the five points. My chocolate gnome sat in the centre of the table. "Hellee Leerroo?" The gnome's voice sounded scared now. "Loorree???"

Marcel said, "We will need a drop of your blood, and one hundred dollars."

I forked over the cash and held out my hand. A blade slashed out like silent lightning. A huge gash appeared across my palm, the flesh pulling back from a deep wound. "Holy fuck!" I shouted as he collected the blood in a stone cup.

Marcel tilted his head back and drank my blood from the cup. He started laughing, and burst into flames.

A unicorn-dragon with golden feathers and silver wings appeared before me, holding the moon in two of its many bronze hands. "Larry," said the dazzling creature, in a dazzling voice. "Put the moon in your heart."

I had to hold up my hands to shield my eyes from the increasing brilliance of the unicorn-dragon. "Why won't the chocolate gnome pronounce my name right?"

The beast started spinning around in a circle like a clock-hand, still holding the moon. She stopped when she pointed at 12. "Seven nineteen sixty-one, Larry."

"What?"

But then the creature was gone and I was lying on the floor with two red eyes looking down at me. "Larry? Are you hurt?"

"I saw a unicorn-dragon. She had a moon."

Marcel grabbed my shoulder with fingers like steel. "This cannot be. You must not have dreams of unicorn-dragons. Not in my den."

"I did!"

Marcel leaned back, his glowing eyes gazing off into despair. "Oh no."

"Hellee Larree!" The gnome shouted with delight. He was standing on the ceiling, upside down.

"What's wrong?" I asked. "Why is the chocolate still haunted? What's wrong with unicorn-dragons?"

"That is not for us to know. We must simply follow the directions of your spirit-guide. Was your unicorn-dragon spinning like a compass? Where did she point in the end?"

"North."

"Ah but there is a problem with going north," Marcel

said, shaking his head sadly.

"Why? What's wrong with going north?"

"Going north will take more of my time, so you will need to give me another two hundred dollars."

I pulled out a wad of bills and peeled off his price. Then Marcel led me outside into the sandy street and hailed a rickshaw and said, "Mr. rickshaw-driver, we must leave the city. Take us north."

The rickshaw driver looked like a lumberjack with a greying beard and a flannel jacket. He trundled us through the dusty streets and we shared water from a leather canteen. After crossing the train tracks the buildings were replaced by palm trees. The dirt road sloped up and the palm trees were replaced by evergreens and birch. Occasionally I would see my chocolate gnome in the branches smiling at me. "Hallaa Lorroo!"

As the sun set I said, "Marcel, what are we looking for?"

"A sign," he said.

And then it came. We passed by a great factory with

brown-painted aluminum siding. Smoke poured out of its smokestacks. The address said 71961. I pointed and said, "That's the number the unicorn-dragon told me in my dream!"

"Then we have reached our destination," Marcel said. "Rickshaw driver! Stop here and let us free."

The rickshaw-driver said, "That'll be five bucks, buddy."

"Here is your payment," Marcel said, and he unsheathed a scimitar and sliced open the drivers' belly. The drivers guts spilled out and he collapsed on the ground, writhing and bleeding. "When you get to Hell, ask the devil for your five bucks, *buddy*."

I said, "Fuck, why'd you kill him?"

"Dead men keep their secrets. Now let us complete the dehaunting of your delicious chocolate."

The gnome appeared amidst the steaming guts and said, "Halla Larraa! Hoolloo Loorrooooo!"

There were two doors into the factory. One said *visitors*, and the other said, *employees*. Marcel said, "Only the employees know the company's secrets. Let us use their door."

I pulled the handle but the door wouldn't budge. "Locked for the night," I said.

"Bastards."

We walked around the perimeter looking for a place to sneak in. A gravel parking lot sprawled out beside the factory like a gravel pancake. Behind it was a great grassy field. In the dim light I saw a dump truck and some people gathering around a big, fresh hole that was dug in the field.

"Let's investigate this commotion," I said. As we approached, the dump truck tilted its bed and spilled its load into the hole. Hundreds of green humanoid bodies spilled from the back of the truck, tumbling like colourful candy into the dark pit. I gasped. "Aliens!"

"I am beginning to grasp the problem," Marcel said. "You brought the chocolate box here with you, did you not?"

I held up the cardboard package that had once held the chocolate gnome.

"What is the address?"

I looked. "71961 Highway Avenue! It's right here!"

"Yes, my friend," Marcel said. "This factory, it is the chocolate factory from which your gnome was birthed. But it is right next to an alien graveyard! So the ghosts of the aliens, if they are not at peace, they begin to haunt nearby desserts. Then they lure the owner of the desserts here, to the scene of the injustice, so you can stop the cycle of alien-cruelty. They are a cry for help."

"What kind of cruelty? How did these aliens die?"

"Let us investigate!"

As we got closer to the giant hole I saw a man in a business suit with a huge wad of bills in his hand. He was laughing and counting his money.

I recognized this strange, night-time money-counter right away. It was the mayor!

I snatched the money from his hand and said, "Mayor Dog! I should have known you were behind this."

He snatched the money back and gave me a confident smile. "Behind what?"

"You're using these alien corpses to haunt the

chocolates in the chocolate factory."

The dump truck drove away and another one pulled up. It tilted its bed, dumping anvils and rocks into the hole on top of the alien corpses. "Larry, you fool. Why would I haunt chocolates? During the last elections I vowed to fight against ghosts, not for them. How would I benefit from haunting chocolates?"

Finally a final dump truck trundled up and dumped its payload: a splashing gush of boiling water, which sent misty steam up into the night, obscuring the stars. The mayor had posed a good question. How did he benefit from haunting my chocolate gnome? Follow the money, Larry.

The gnome appeared on the mayor's head and said, "Hellow Larrow!"

Who benefited from haunted chocolates? Follow the money. Only Marcel had benefited financially from the possessed dessert. I looked at my consort and his red glowing eyes. I said, "Maybe Marcel is splitting the money with you."

"Ha!" The mayor said. "You think his measly fee can

pay for these dump trucks? And the alien corpses? What kind of scheme is that?"

I fingered my lip and scoured my brain. The cold night air felt good and helped me think. Why were they bringing alien corpses out here? Why were they also dumping anvils and hot water on the corpses? What happens when you take corpses, apply pressure, and increase the temperature?

"Alien oil!" I exclaimed. "You're making alien oil."

"Quite right," the mayor proudly admitted. "We're taking alien corpses and processing them into alien oil, which is more potent than Earthly oil. I had to pay the chocolate factory to let me use their back yard. When the dead, angry aliens started haunting the nearby chocolates I decided to invest in a little side-business: my friend Marcel here has made lots of money by pretending to be a dehaunter, and he splits that money with me."

"No, not Marcel!" I said.

"It is true," said the backstabbing bastard who I once called a dehaunter. He gave Mayor Dog half the money

I'd paid him and stood beside the mayor. "I am no dehaunter. Merely a backstabbing, lying, murdering, red-eyed computer programmer who sometimes poses as a dehaunter. I am not sorry. I had fun stealing your money, and I am still having fun knowing that the aliens will soon take you away from us forever."

"Aliens? Why would they help you by kidnapping me? Clearly you're enemies to the aliens, who you've murdered."

The mayor said, "Aliens have class wars just like us. The rich aliens give us the poor aliens so we can kill them and make alien oil out of them. In return, we give them our losers and suckers so they can use them as sex slaves or make human oil out of them."

Then a beam of light appeared above my head, enveloping me in an electric glow. An alien spaceship beamed me and my chocolate gnome into their ship. Then they flew into space, and we became their sex-slaves.

ABOUT THE AUTHOR:

Matt Payne writes comedic novels and adventure novels. He lives in Ottawa.

www.ingramcontent.com/pod-product-compliance
Lightning Source LLC
Chambersburg PA
CBHW031845170626
46807CB00004B/1629